FRANÉ LESSAC

CARIBBEAN ALPHABET

TAMBOURINE BOOKS · NEW YORK

Copyright © 1989 by Frané Lessac

First published in Great Britain by the Macmillan Press Ltd

Library of Congress Cataloging in Publication Data

Lessac, Frané. Caribbean alphabet/Frané Lessac. — 1st U.S. ed. p. cm. Summary: Presents an alphabet of

images from the Caribbean, such as hibiscus, mangoes, and reggae. 1. Caribbean, English-speaking — Description and

travel — Dictionaries, Juvenile. 2. Caribbean, English-speaking — Dictionaries, Juvenile. [1. Caribbean Area. 2. Alphabet.]

I. Title. F2130.L47 1994 421'.1[E] — dc20 93-15833 CIP AC ISBN 0-688-12952-8. — ISBN 0-688-12953-6 (lib. bdg.)

First U.S. edition, 1994

1 3 5 7 9 10 8 6 4 2

For Arthur and Rosemary

airport   arrivals   airplane   agouti

boat birds breadfruit bananas

cricket coconut cat cows

donkeys dolphins dasheen

egrets eggs estuary eels

fort   fisherman   frogs   flowers

goats grass gate gazebo

house hummingbirds hibiscus

island iguanas inlet

jump-up Junkanoo

kids kites kittens knots

lightning lighthouse limbo lizards

mountains   market   mangoes   melons

nutmeg   nets   nuts   nests

ocean   orange   oars octopus

pirate   pelican   pineapples   pawpaws

quay   queen-conch

rainbow Rastafarians reggae radio

steelband sand starfish seashells

tourists towels turtles treasure

university uniforms umbrellas

village view volcano valley

whale   wharf   watermelons   waves

x marks the spot

yellow   yacht

zoo zebra zookeeper zzzz

GLOSSARY

Agouti
A furry, rabbit-sized rodent of the West Indies.

Breadfruit
A tropical fruit that, when baked, tastes like bread.

Dasheen
The taro plant, whose root is a popular Caribbean vegetable.

Egret
A bird of the heron family.

Hibiscus
A colorful flowering plant.

Iguana
A tropical lizard.

Junkanoo
A Caribbean festival celebrated over the Christmas holidays on various islands, often featuring the folk dance known as Jump-up.

Pawpaw
The sweet fruit of the papaya tree.

Queen-conch
A sea snail prized for its shell.

Rastafarians
Followers of a Jamaican cultural and religious movement.

Reggae
An internationally popular Jamaican style of music.

Steelband
Musicians playing instruments first fashioned in Trinidad out of old barrels and oil drums.